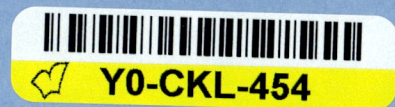

For Henry and Marie

DIAL BOOKS FOR YOUNG READERS • An imprint of Penguin Random House LLC
1745 Broadway, New York, New York 10019

First published in the United States of America by Dial Books yor Young Readers, an imprint of Penguin Random House LLC, 2025 • Copyright © 2025 by Adam Rex

Penguin Random House values and supports copyright. Copyright fuels creativity, encourages diverse voices, promotes free speech, and creates a vibrant culture. Thank you for buying an authorized edition of this book and for complying with copyright laws by not reproducing, scanning, or distributing any part of it in any form without permission. You are supporting writers and allowing Penguin Random House to continue to publish books for every reader. Please note that no part of this book may be used or reproduced in any manner for the purpose of training artificial intelligence technologies or systems.

Dial Books for Young Readers & colophon are trademarks of Penguin Random House LLC
The Penguin colophon is a registered trademark of Penguin Books Limited.
Visit us online at PenguinRandomHouse.com.

Library of Congress Cataloging-in-Publication Data is available.

Manufactured in China • ISBN 9780593699324 • TOPL • 10 9 8 7 6 5 4 3 2 1

This book was edited by Kate Harrison, copyedited and proofread by Regina Castillo, and designed by Jason Henry. The production was supervised by Jayne Ziemba, Nicole Kiser, and Hansi Weedagama. Text set in Museo Slab.

The art in this book was drawn and painted digitally in Procreate and Photoshop.

The publisher does not have any control over and does not assume any responsibility for author or third-party websites or their content.

HO

by Adam Rex

DIAL BOOKS FOR YOUNG READERS

Junior Junior was born in a big house on the side of a mountain...

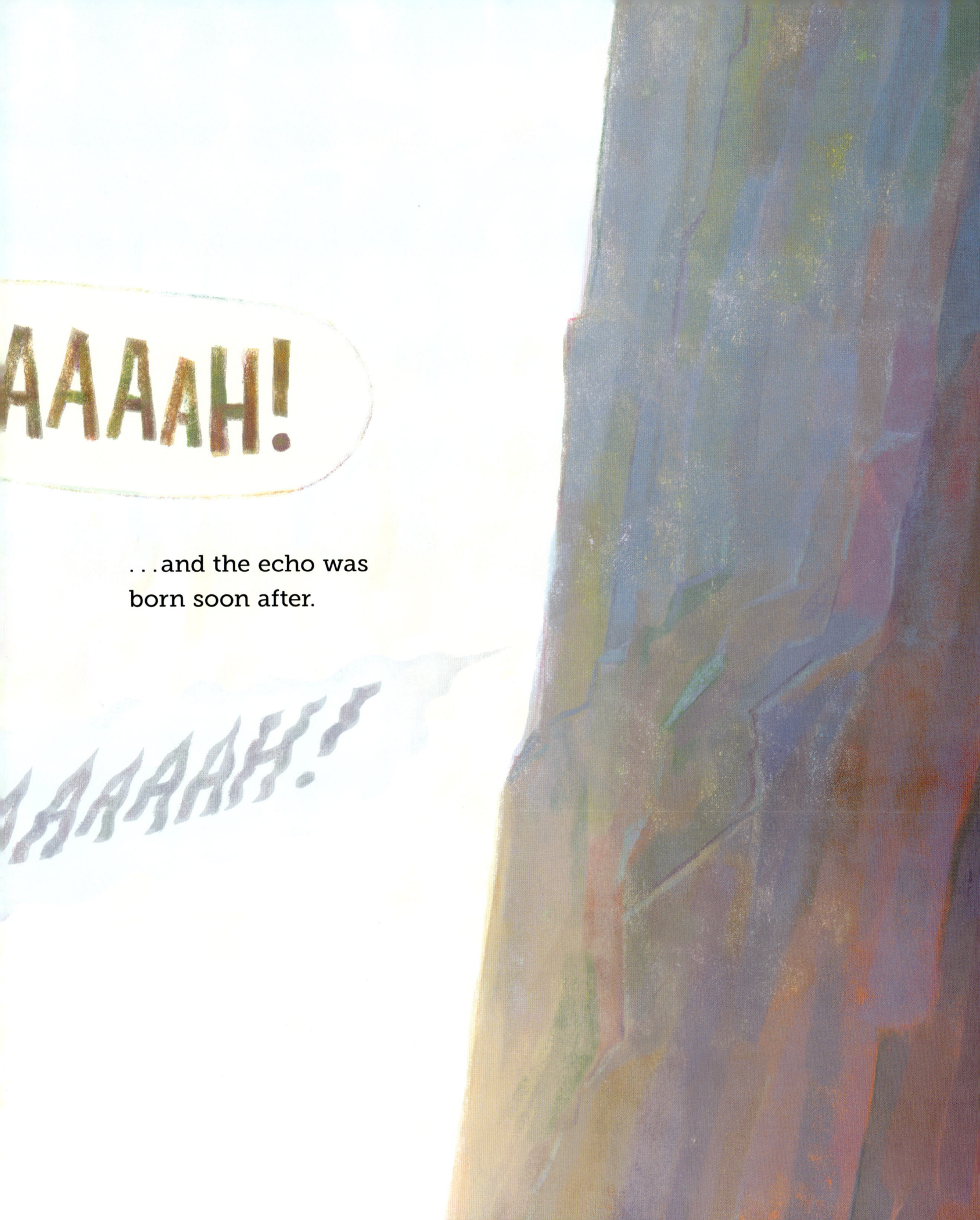

AAAAH!

...and the echo was born soon after.

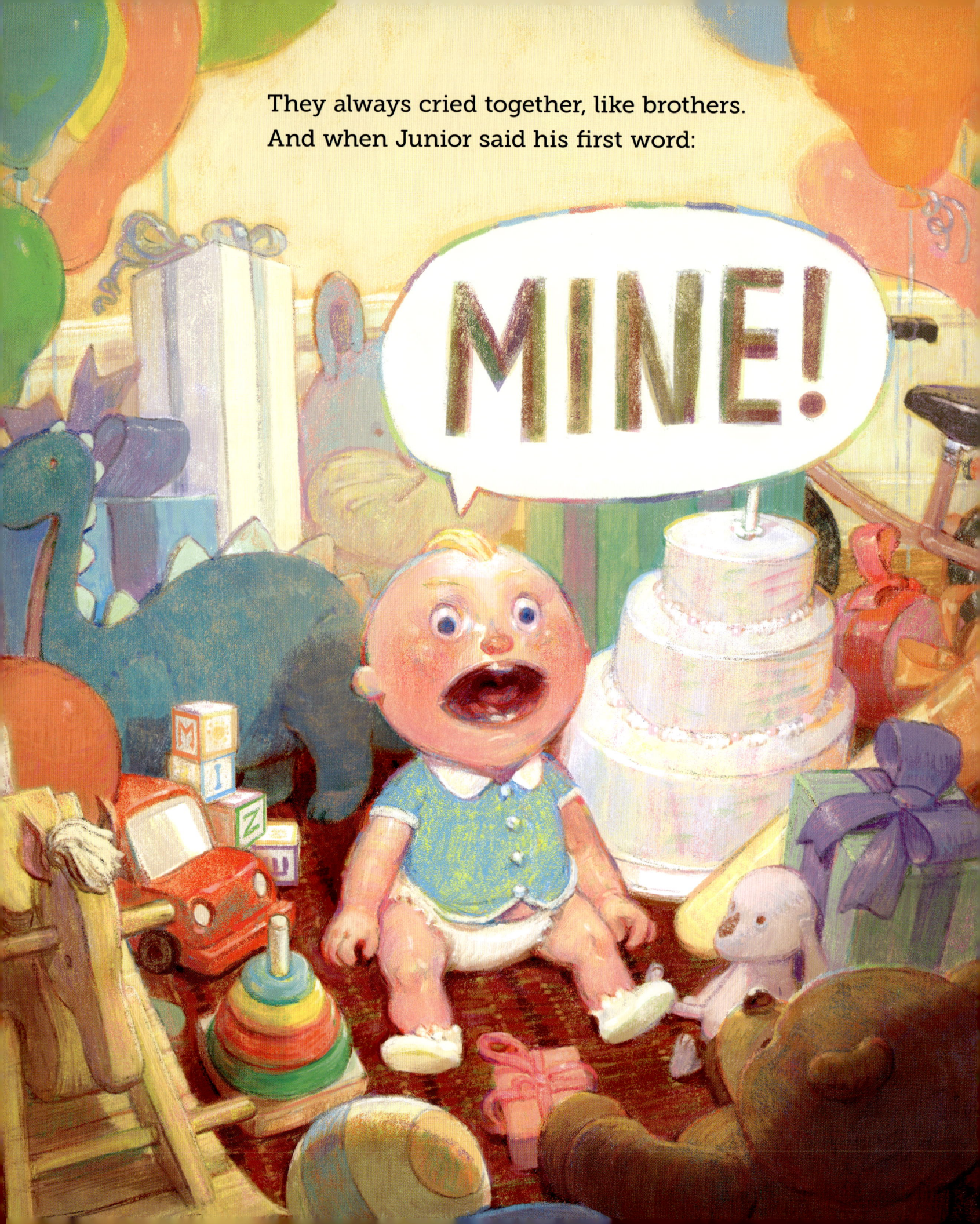

He didn't think he liked that boy who lived across the valley.

But after one difficult day, when Nanny said,
Junior must eat his blueberries,
and,
Junior mustn't throw his blueberries,
and later,
Junior must help find the blueberries,
the boy ran to the window and shouted:

JUNIOR JUNIOR IS THE GREATEST IN THE WORLD!

JUNIOR JUNIOR IS THE GREATEST IN THE WORLD! agreed the echo.

IN THE WORLD!

Oh.

After that, the boy and the echo were friends.

They talked all day, and sang songs at bedtime.

JUNIOR JUNIOR IS THE SMARTEST!

JUNIOR JUNIOR IS THE SMARTEST!

(It was great.)

OTHER CHILDREN ARE A BOTHER!

OTHER CHILDREN ARE A BOTHER!

(Still, it's lonely when your only friend is so far away.)

WOW, HE'S ONE TERRIFIC ARTIST!

WOW, HE'S ONE TERRIFIC ARTIST!

PLUS HE HAS A FAMOUS FA—

Please stop shouting, said someone.

You're new, he told the girl.

Yes, we just moved here from—

Wasn't that an excellent song?
asked Junior. I wrote it myself.

Hmm, said the girl.

I'll teach you so you can sing it, too.

I...can't, said the girl.
I need to unpack my shovels.

Junior frowned.

He said, My house is bigger than your house.

The girl said, That's true.

At school I am the smartest, said Junior.

Hmm.

Junior wasn't sure about all these *Hmms*.

He said, When *I* grow up, I will be an astronaut like my father, and rocket to the stars. I'll visit that one first, because it's the brightest.

The girl looked.
That's a planet, she said.

Junior flinched.

Is not.

Does it look a little reddish? asked the girl. It might be Mars.

Junior's hair felt hot.

Ahem. I THINK I know what I am talking about. My FATHER is an ASTRONAUT.

The girl shoveled sand.

You should look it up, she said.

Junior frowned all through bath time. Before bed he called from his window,

STARS AREN'T MARS!

STARS AREN'T MARS! the echo agreed.

It was nice to talk to someone sensible.

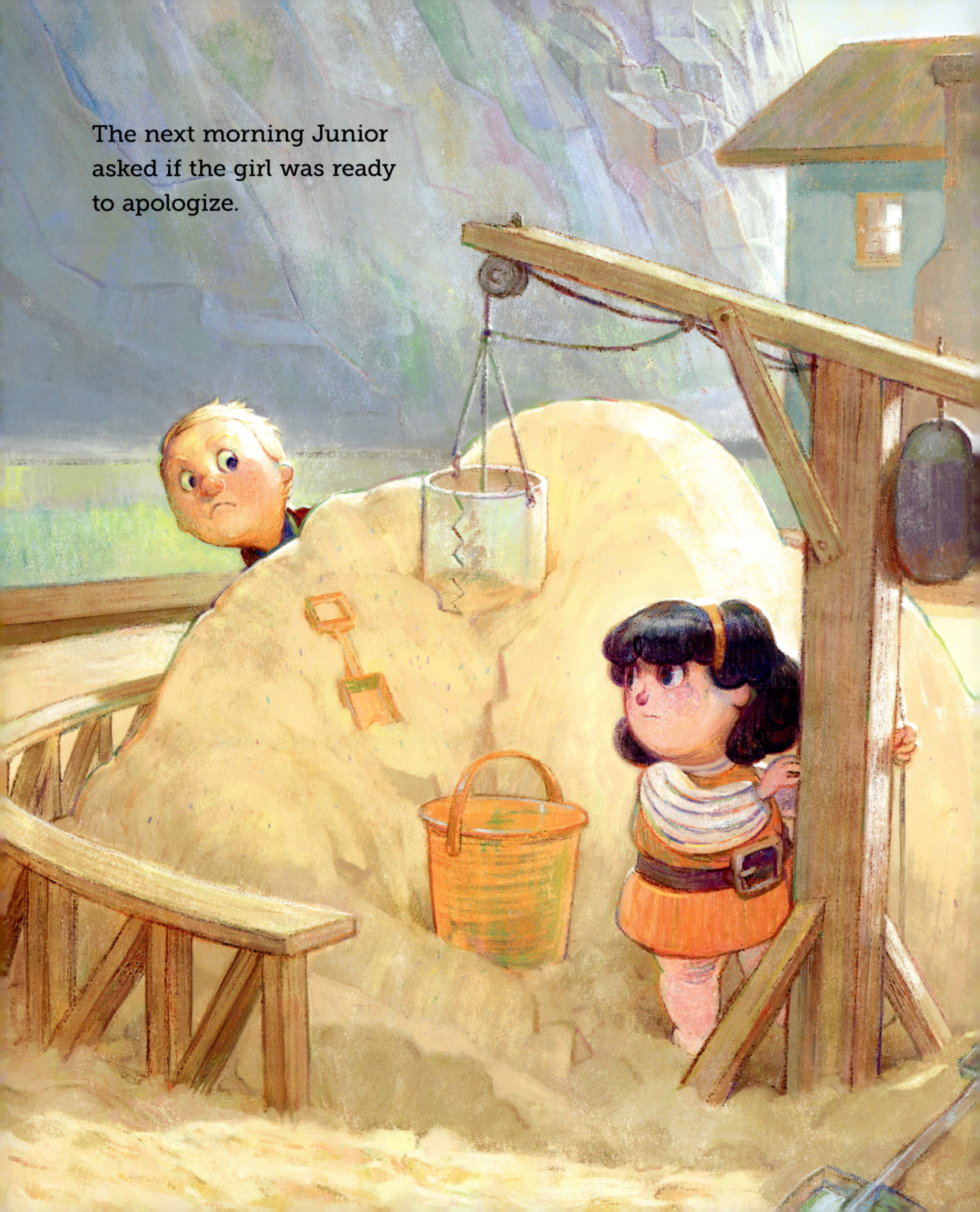

The next morning Junior asked if the girl was ready to apologize.

Apologize? For what?

It's rude to disagree, said Junior.

I don't agree with that, said the girl.

Stars aren't Mars! Junior shouted.
I'm right and you're wrong!

The girl dusted her hands.

There's nothing wrong with
being wrong, she said. I admit
it when I am. But I'm not.

Junior shivered with anger. He stomped up to his balcony and shouted:

Finally he went back inside

and read a book about Mars.

And then he decided to run away from home.

MARCO! he called.

MARCO! the echo answered.

They called and climbed until they met in the middle.

On a little bridge over the river, Junior met his echo.

He was exactly as he'd imagined—handsome and smart-looking.

Junior said, What do you want to do?

What do you want to do? asked the echo.

Junior suggested they throw rocks. Rocks in the river. Rocks in the trees.

When one rock of Junior's landed blandly in some ferns, he said, That was a great throw.

That was a great throw, agreed the echo. Though it hadn't been.

Hmm.

Let's...stand on one leg, said Junior.

Let's stand on one leg.

And hoot like an owl, said Junior.
HOOT HOOT HOOT!

HOOT HOOT HOOT!

Let's hop! And flap our arms!

Those were good ideas! said Junior.

Those were good ideas!

Is that what you really think?

Is that what you really think?

Junior sighed. How tiresome.

After a moment he added, I know that star was Mars.

I know that star was Mars, said the echo.

Before you said it wasn't.

Before you *said it wasn't.*

Hmph, said Junior. And by the way the echo grunted, Junior could tell he was the sort of fool who always had to be right about everything.

Silly—there was nothing wrong with being wrong.

He squinted at the mountain.

There's this girl in the house next to me,
he said. The echo had the same problem.

SHE ARGUES! ARGUES!

Yes, argues! Junior said. Like she doesn't know
what's good for her!

Good for her! said the echo.

Then it was quiet.

Hmm, Junior thought.

Good for her.

I'm going back home, he called.
The echo was too.

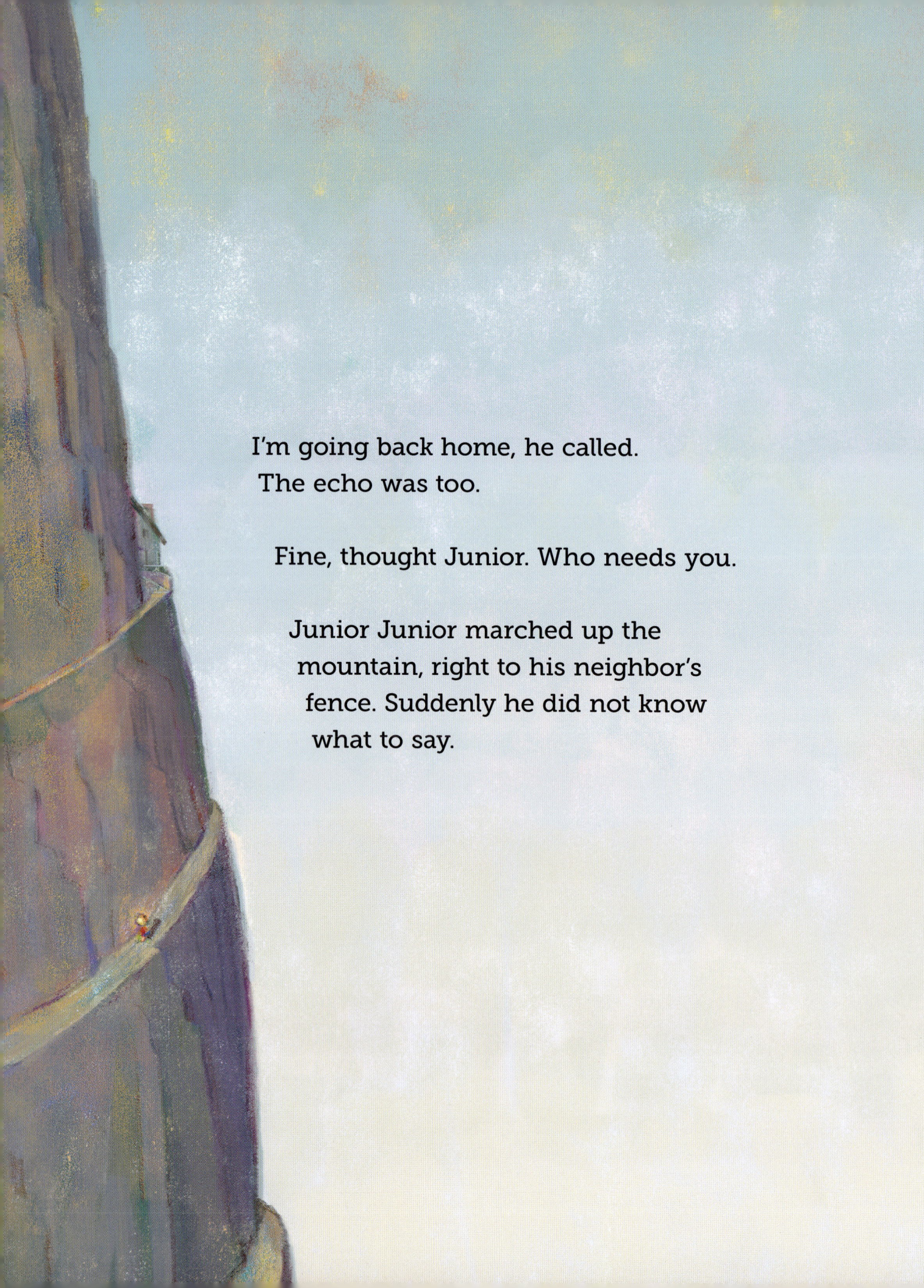

Fine, thought Junior. Who needs you.

Junior Junior marched up the mountain, right to his neighbor's fence. Suddenly he did not know what to say.

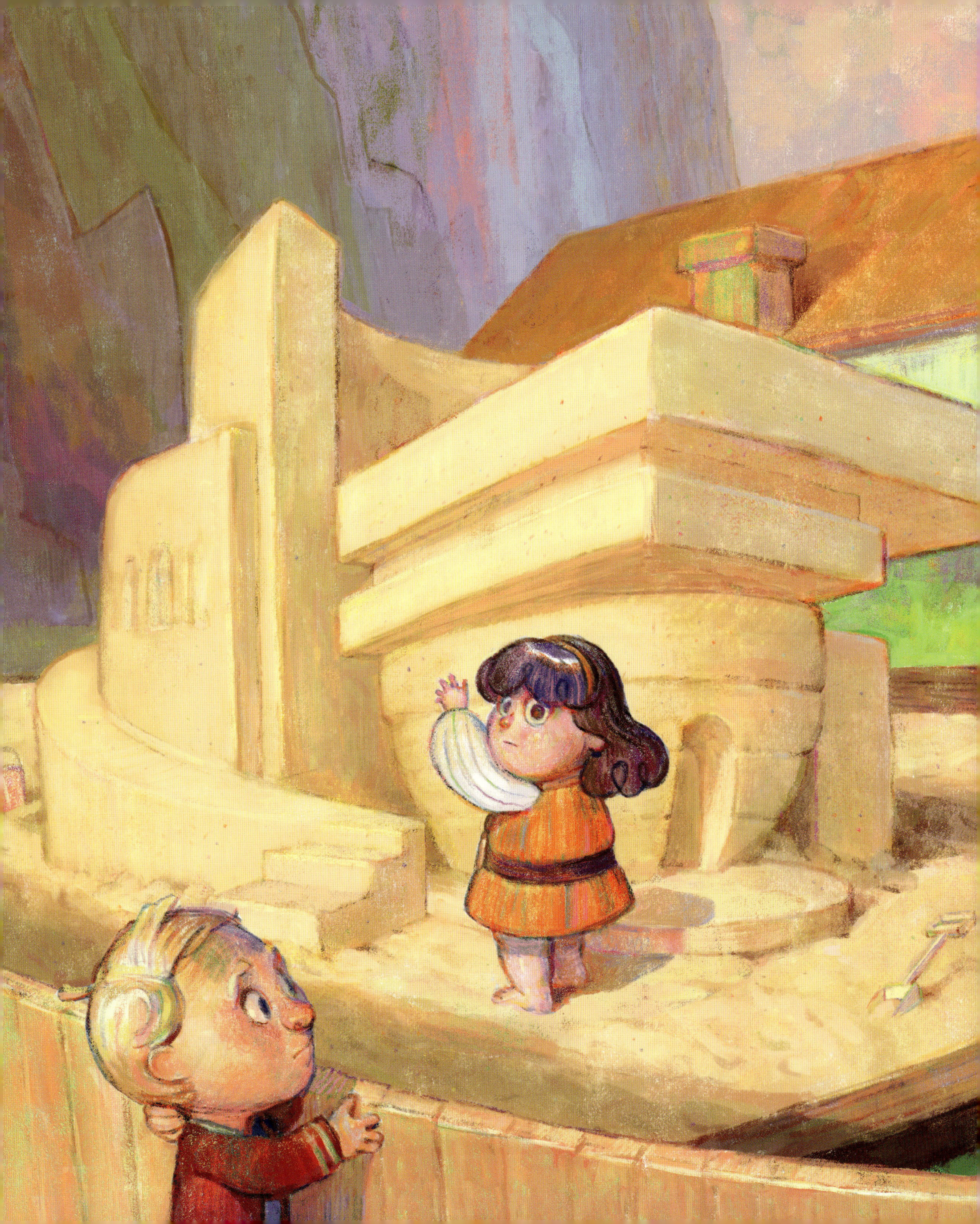

Um. I like your sandcastle.

The girl looked surprised. Thank you, she said.

And...said Junior, and I shouldn't have called you an idiot!

No, she agreed. You shouldn't have.

Junior looked at his feet.

Wanna talk about planets? Since you know about planets?

The girl said, I really want to finish my sandcastle.

Right. Um. What's your name?

Sandy.

Junior was not going to make the best sandcastle. He thought that might be okay.

He told Sandy, I'm glad you're here.

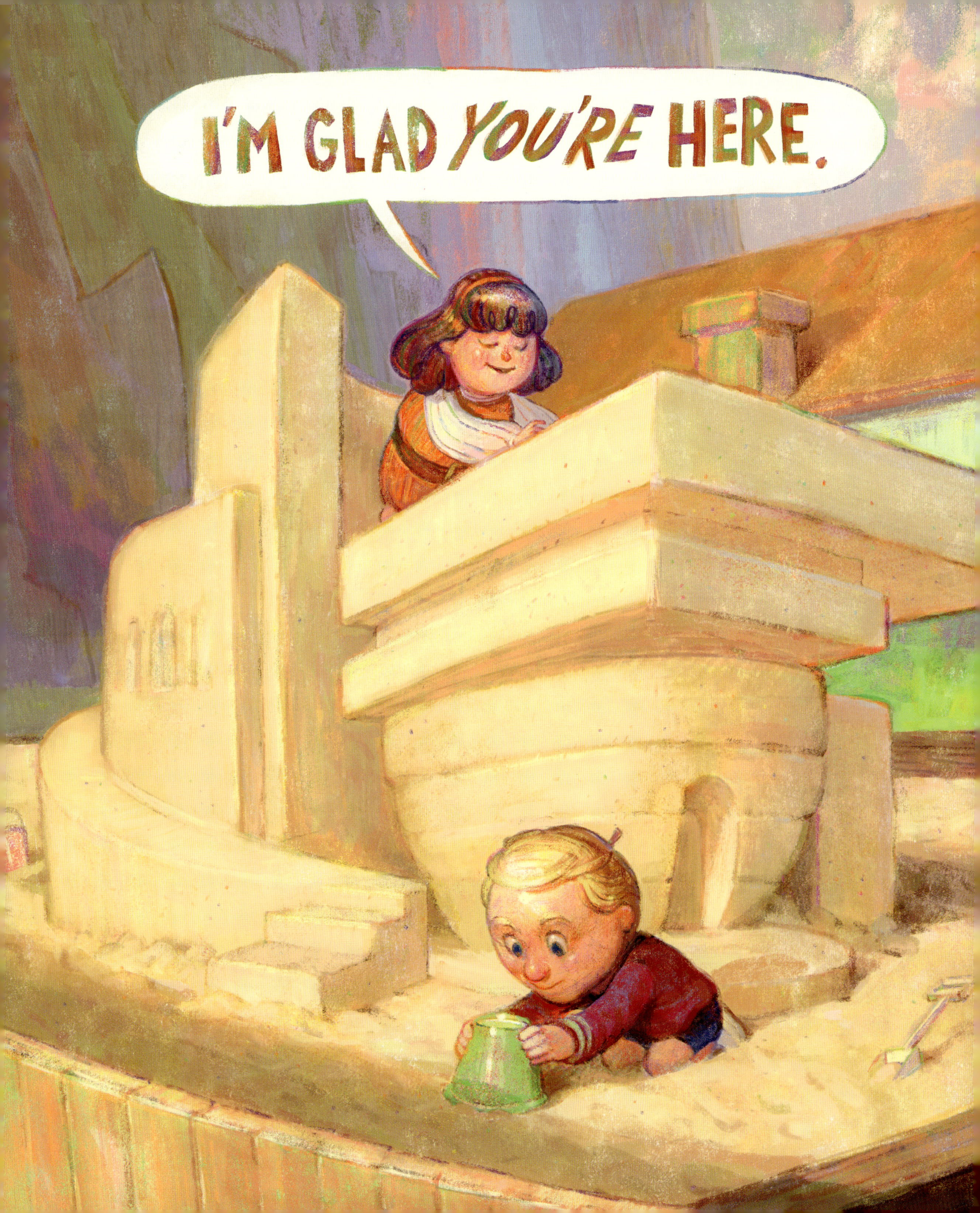
I'M GLAD *YOU'RE* HERE.

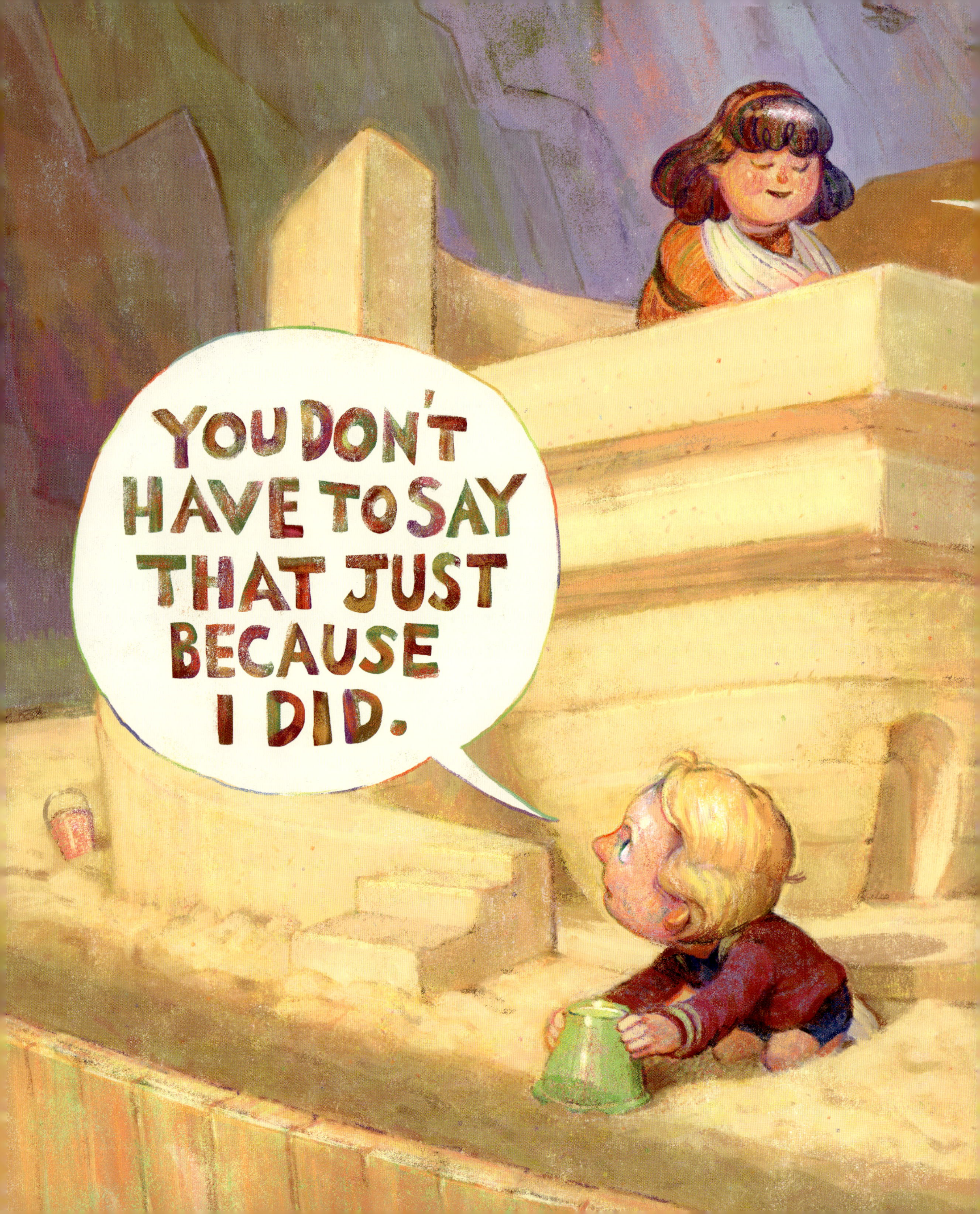
YOU DON'T HAVE TO SAY THAT JUST BECAUSE I DID.

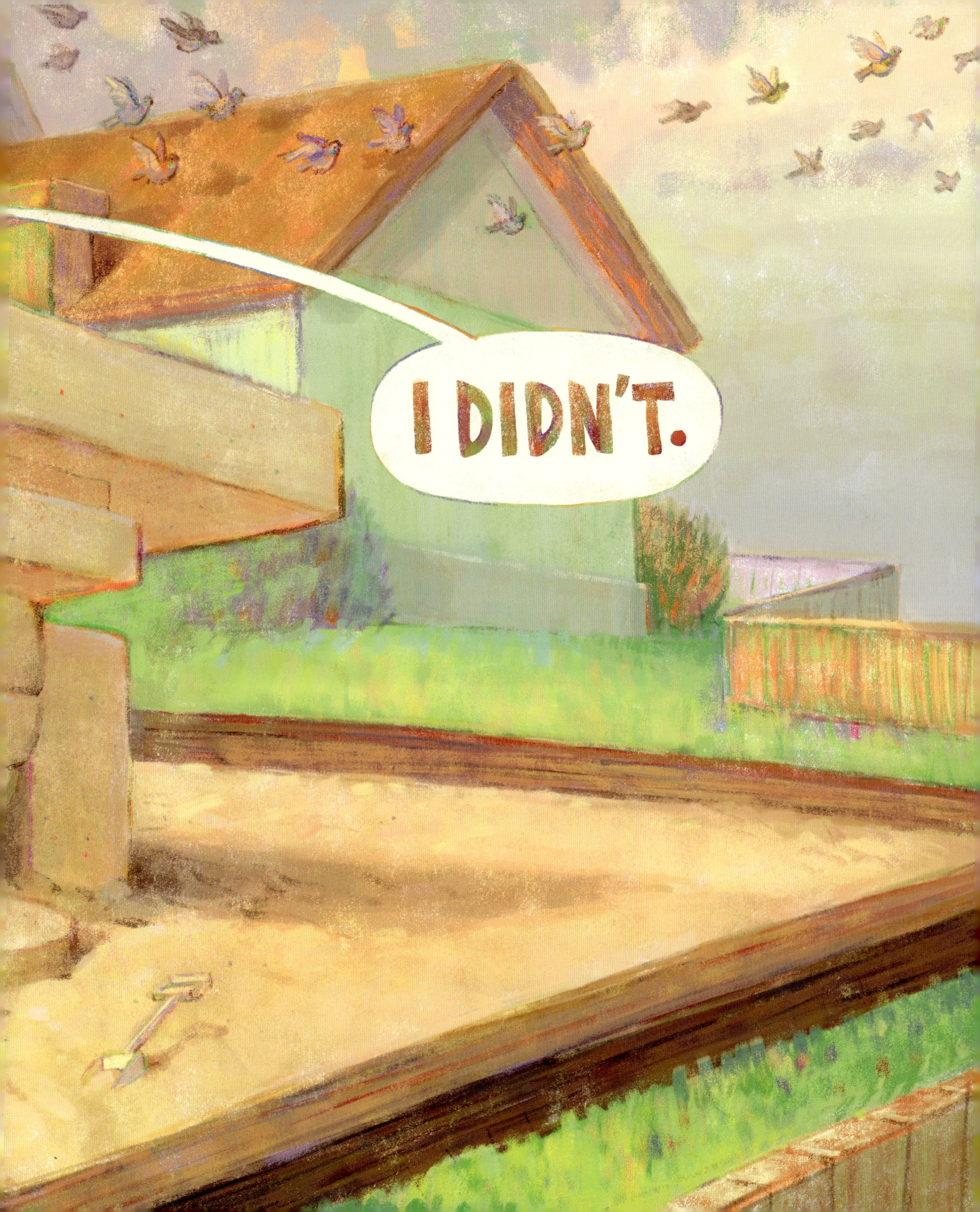
I DIDN'T.

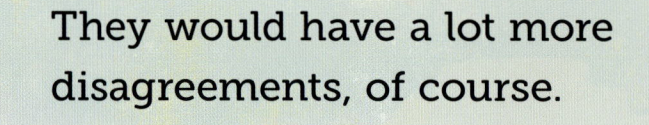

They would have a lot more disagreements, of course.

OF COURSE!

But after that day, they were friends to the end.

THE END!